Barnyard Fun

BY

Maureen Wright

ILLUSTRATED BY

Paul
Rátz de Tagyos

SCHOLASTIC INC.

ISBN 978−0−545−67711−0

Text copyright © 2013 by Maureen Wright.
Illustrations copyright © 2013 by Paul Rátz de Tagyos. All rights reserved.
Published by Scholastic Inc., 557 Broadway, New York, NY 10012,
by arrangement with Amazon Children's Publishing. SCHOLASTIC and
associated logos are trademarks and/or registered trademarks of Scholastic Inc.

12 11 10 9 8 7 6 5 4 3 2 1   14 15 16 17 18 19/0

Printed in the U.S.A.   40

First Scholastic printing, March 2014

The illustrations are rendered in markers on Bienfang marker paper.
Book design by Anahid Hamparian
Editor: Margery Cuyler

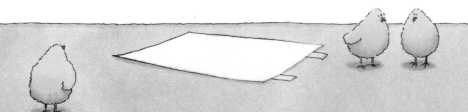

When Sheep found out it was April One, he said, "It's time to have some fun!"

Sheep set the alarm an hour ahead.
It woke up Rooster in his bed.

Rooster crowed, "It's morning time!

Everybody rise and shine!"

"April Fools!"

the old sheep said.

"What are you doing out of bed?"

When Sheep found out it was April One,
he said, "I've only just begun!"

Sheep took a can and closed the lid,
then ran behind the hay and hid.

Dog searched for something good to eat.

"Hey, look!" he said.
"My favorite treat."

Suddenly three snakes popped out!
The young dog barked and jumped about.

"April Fools!"

the old sheep said.

"Are you still waiting to be fed?"

When Sheep found out it was April One,
he said, "This joke is lots of fun!"

Sheep took a box—flat and wide—
and frosted both the top and sides.

The box looked like a pretty cake.
No one knew that it was fake!

Pig grabbed a fork and took a bite.
Sheep burst out laughing at the sight.

"April Fools!"

the old sheep said.

"I see your face is blushing red!"

When Sheep found out it was April One,
he said, "I think I'm almost done."

"Let's play the game Connect-the-Dots,
using all of Cow's black spots."

Duck walked by and hollered, "Wow!
Check out the spots on the silly cow!"

"What?" said Cow. "How can that be?
Look at the smiley face on me!"

"April Fools!"

the old sheep said.

He laughed and shook his woolly head.

When it was time to go to bed,
the horse looked down at Sheep and said,
"Aren't you hot in your coat, my friend?
The Farmer forgot to shear you again.

A haircut would look so nice on you.
I'll trim your coat if you'd like me to."

The sheep said, "Thanks!
That sounds just fine.
I'm hot and stuffy all the time."

The shaver *buzzzzzzzzzzed* up and down.
"Hold still," said Horse. "Don't move around."

The spotted cow mooed low and deep.

Small chicks chuckled, "Cheep—cheep—cheep."

The dog's tail wiggled like a snake.

Rooster laughed till his belly ached.

Pig's tail twirled like a curly noodle.

"April Fools!" they yelled to the brand-new . . .

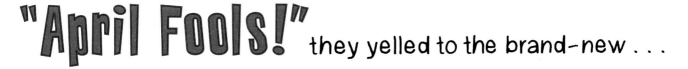

Poodle!